This book belongs to

Franklin's Holiday Treasury

Franklin is a trademark of Kids Can Press Ltd.

Franklin's Holiday Treasury

© 2002 Contextx Inc. and Brenda Clark Illustrator Inc.

This book includes the following stories:
Franklin's Halloween first published in 1996
Franklin's Valentines first published in 1998
Franklin's Christmas Gift first published in 1998
Franklin's Thanksgiving first published in 2001

All text © 1996, 1998, 2001 Contextx Inc.
All illustrations © 1996, 1998, 2001 Brenda Clark Illustrator Inc.

Franklin's Valentines and *Franklin's Thanksgiving* written by Sharon Jennings.
Franklin's Halloween interior illustrations prepared with the assistance
of Muriel Hughes Wood.
Franklin's Valentines, *Franklin's Christmas Gift* and *Franklin's Thanksgiving*
interior illustrations prepared with the assistance of Shelley Southern.

Kids Can Press acknowledges the financial support of the Ontario Arts Council,
the Canada Council for the Arts and the Government of Canada, through the
BPIDP, for our publishing activity.

Published in Canada by
Kids Can Press Ltd.
29 Birch Avenue
Toronto, ON M4V 1E2

Published in the U.S. by
Kids Can Press Ltd.
2250 Military Road
Tonawanda, NY 14150

www.kidscanpress.com

Printed in Hong Kong by Wing King Tong Company Limited

CM 02 0 9 8 7 6 5 4 3 2 1

National Library of Canada Cataloguing in Publication Data

Bourgeois, Paulette
    Franklin's holiday treasury

Contents: *Franklin's Christmas gift* – *Franklin's Halloween* – *Franklin's Thanksgiving* – *Franklin's Valentines.*

ISBN 1-55337-045-7

1. Children's stories, Canadian (English). I. Clark, Brenda. II. Title.

PS8553.O85477F863 2001   jC813'.54   C2001-902831-8
PZ7.B6654Fxi 2001

Kids Can Press is a *Corus*™ Entertainment company

❦ Franklin's ❦
HOLIDAY
Treasury

Paulette Bourgeois • Brenda Clark

Kids Can Press

Contents

Franklin's Halloween

FRANKLIN could count by twos and tie his shoes. He knew the days of the week, the months of the year and the holidays in every season. Today was October 31. It was Halloween! Franklin could hardly wait for tonight's costume party. Everyone would be there.

11

Franklin and his friends had talked about the party for weeks. There would be games, prizes and even a parade. Best of all, there would be a haunted house.

"I think there'll be bats and spiders," said Franklin.

"And skeletons," added Beaver.

Rabbit shivered. "My sister says she saw a real ghost in there last year."

"That's silly, Rabbit," said Beaver. "There are no *real* ghosts."

All of Franklin's friends were excited
because of the costume contest.

Franklin wasn't sure what he was going to wear. He'd tried on everything in his dress-up trunk, but nothing seemed quite right.

Beaver and Goose were keeping their costumes secret.

"Try to find us at the party," they giggled.

Fox was also mysterious about what he was going to be.

"Look for something gruesome," he said.

That gave Franklin an idea. He would be something creepy.

17

It took Franklin more than an hour to make his costume.

As soon as it was done, he sneaked up behind his father and tapped him on the shoulder.

"Trick or treat," said Franklin.

"Ahhhh!" gasped his father. "Who are you?"

In his deepest, spookiest voice, Franklin answered, "It's me. Franklinstein!"

On the way to town, Franklin tried to guess who was inside each costume.

"At least I don't have to worry about finding Bear," said Franklin. "He's always a ghost."

By the time Franklin and his parents arrived, the party had started.

Franklin spotted a ghost at the apple-bobbing and hurried towards him. "Hello, Bear," Franklin said.

"Whooo!" answered the ghost.

"That's good, Bear," said Franklin. "You sound really scary."

Franklin bobbed for an apple. Then he ran to the pumpkin toss. It was his favourite game because he always won a treat.

Franklin's bag was almost full by the time the judges announced the costume contest. While everyone lined up for the parade, Franklin tried to find more of his friends. He thought he recognized Beaver and Goose. But where was Fox?

They marched around the building twice.

Franklin made horrible monster sounds and shuffled with stiff, straight legs. He won a prize for being the best green monster.

There was only one more thing to do – go into the haunted house.

"You first," said Beaver, pushing Franklin towards the door.

It creaked open. A skeleton rattled. Chains clanged. There were moans. Franklin stepped on something crunchy.

Suddenly, a big hairy hand reached out of the darkness.

Franklin's heart beat hard and fast. But before he could scream, a light was flicked on.

"Trick or treat!" shouted Mr. Mole.

Franklin looked around nervously. Then he laughed. The hairy hand was only Mr. Mole's mop.

"Here's a treat for braving the haunted house," said Mr. Mole. "A ghost came before you. He got so scared he flew away."

"But Bear can't fly," said Franklin.

"It wasn't Bear," explained Mr. Mole. "Bear is home sick with a nasty cold."

Franklin shuddered. "If Bear wasn't the ghost, then who was?"

He ran back to his friends, who were waiting in line for the haunted house.

"Was it that scary?" asked Fox. "You look like you've seen a ghost."

"Maybe I did," said Franklin. He told them what Mr. Mole had said.

"You mean that Bear was never here?" asked Beaver.

Franklin shook his head.

The ghost flew over them. It swooped low and called, "Whooo!"

Rabbit twitched. "So what is white, says 'Whooo' and flies?"

"A real ghost," answered Goose. "Run!"

Franklin was about to follow when he saw a feather floating down.

"Stop!" he shouted. "I think I know *whooo* the ghost is."

Franklin showed them the feather. "Look. It must be Mr. Owl."

Even Rabbit giggled when he realized the trick their teacher had played.

By the end of the party, everyone's bag was full.
"Poor Bear," said Raccoon. "No treats for him."

"We could share our treats with Bear," suggested
Franklin.

All the friends agreed. They each put some treats
into a bag. Then they walked to Bear's house and left
the bag on the doorstep.

"Trick *and* treat!" they called.

On the way home, Franklin looked into his treat bag.

"Goodness!" said his mother. "You have enough there to last until next Halloween."

"Maybe," said Franklin, sampling a few. But secretly he hoped the treats would last until the end of the week.

Franklin's Valentines

FRANKLIN could count to ten and back again. He knew the days of the week, the months of the year and the holidays in every season. Today was Valentine's Day, and Franklin was counting the valentines he'd made for his friends. He wanted to be sure he hadn't forgotten anyone.

41

"Hurry up, Franklin," said his mother. "You'll miss the school bus!"

Franklin rushed to find his hat and mittens and boots. He tossed his valentines into his bag.

"I'm going!" called Franklin, and he hurried out the door.

At school, Mr. Owl gave the class a valentine spelling bee and valentine arithmetic problems. But everyone was too excited about the Valentine's Day party to think about work.

Franklin whispered to Bear, "I can't believe we have to wait until after lunch to give out our cards."

"I can't believe we have to wait until after lunch for the goodies," Bear whispered back.

At last, it was time for the party.

"You may get your valentines now," said Mr. Owl.

Franklin grabbed his bag and reached inside. He pulled out his hat, and he pulled out his mittens. He pulled out a ball and a scrunched-up piece of homework. Then he held his bag upside down and shook it.

"What's wrong?" asked Bear.

"My valentines! They're gone!" cried Franklin.

After Franklin looked everywhere, Mr. Owl let him phone home. Franklin waited and waited while his mother searched.

"I'm so sorry, Franklin," she finally said. "I found your valentines outside in a puddle of slush. The cards are ruined."

Franklin blinked away tears. He gave the phone to Mr. Owl and ran out of the room.

Mr. Owl found Franklin in the cloakroom.

"There you are, Franklin," he said. "Your friends are waiting. We can't start the party without you."

"I don't belong at the party," replied Franklin. "I don't have any valentines to give."

"I know," said Mr. Owl. "Your mother told me what happened. And I told the class."

Franklin moaned. "I guess no one's going to give me a valentine now."

"Hmmm," said Mr. Owl. "If Bear lost his valentines, would you decide not to give him a card?"

"I'd never do that!" exclaimed Franklin. "Bear is my friend."

"Maybe Bear feels the same way about you," replied Mr. Owl.

Franklin thought about that.

"Maybe," he said. He cheered up a little.

Franklin and Mr. Owl went back to the classroom.

Franklin watched as his friends delivered
their cards.

As the pile of valentines in front of him
grew bigger and bigger, Franklin felt sadder and
sadder. There were so many, and he had none
to give in return.

He sighed as he opened Bear's card.

"What's wrong, Franklin?" asked Bear.
"Don't you like my card?"

"I do! But I feel bad because I don't have
one for you," said Franklin.

"Oh that's all right," said Bear. "I don't
need a valentine to know you're my friend."

Franklin smiled.

Everyone gathered around as Franklin opened his other cards.

"Mine's a turtle cut-out," said Snail.

"Mine's a turtle poem," said Goose.

"And I made up a turtle riddle," said Fox.

"These are great!" exclaimed Franklin. "I just wish I had my valentines for all of you!"

"I just wish we could start eating all these goodies," replied Bear.

Everybody laughed.

That night, Franklin told his parents about the party.

"It sounds as if you have some very good friends," said Franklin's father.

"I sure do!" agreed Franklin. "Next year, I'm going to make them extra-special valentines!"

"Well, you've got a whole year to get ready," replied his mother.

"I don't know if I can wait a whole year," said Franklin.

61

The next morning, Franklin's mother found him at his table, writing and drawing and cutting and folding.

"What are you making?" she asked.

"It's a surprise," Franklin answered.

His mother smiled. "Well, hurry up. You'll miss the bus."

But Franklin didn't hurry. He wrapped his
artwork carefully and placed the package in his
bag. He made sure that all the buckles were
done up tight. Then he hugged the bag to his
chest and went out the door.

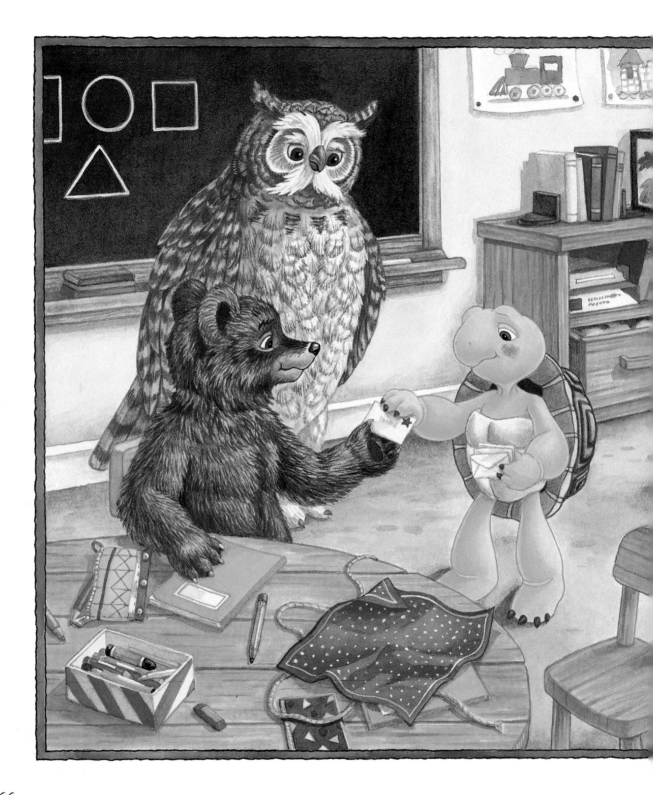

As soon as Franklin got to school, he opened his package and gave everyone a card.

"What are you doing, Franklin?" asked Beaver. "Valentine's Day was yesterday."

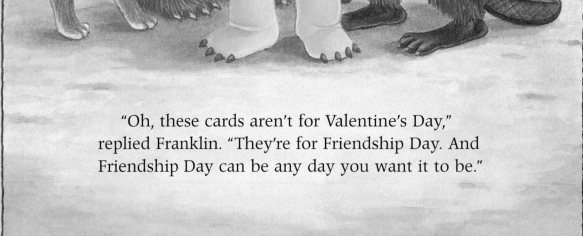

"Oh, these cards aren't for Valentine's Day,"
replied Franklin. "They're for Friendship Day. And
Friendship Day can be any day you want it to be."

Franklin's Christmas Gift

FRANKLIN loved Christmas. He could name all of Santa's reindeer. He could tie ribbons into bows and play "Silent Night" on his recorder.

Franklin liked to give presents and to receive them. But this year he couldn't decide what to give to the Christmas toy drive.

Every December the students in Mr. Owl's class donated toys for needy families. The toys could be new or carefully used.

When Mr. Owl put out the collection box, everyone was excited. They had three days to choose the perfect gifts to give.

That evening Franklin dug through his toys.
He picked up a shiny red car.

"I remember this," he said, wheeling it around.
"Vroom!"

Next, Franklin pulled out a stuffed elephant
and held her tight.

"I wondered where you'd gone!" he cried.

Then Franklin found his best green marble. It had been missing for weeks.

"Fantastic!" he shouted.

Franklin loved his marbles. He had won every marble in his collection, and each one was beautiful.

Franklin picked through the rest of the toys. He decided to keep everything but a rusty truck with a missing wheel.

Franklin asked his father to help him fix the truck.

"We can try," said his father. "But it won't look new or even gently used."

"It's all I have. Everything else is too special to give away."

"I'd like you to think about that," said Franklin's father. "Christmas is a time to be generous."

The next day at school, Franklin asked his friends what they were giving.

Beaver was donating her big book of questions and answers.

"I already know all the answers," she boasted.

"I'm giving a puzzle," said Bear. "I only did it once."

Franklin frowned. "I'm giving a truck ... I think."

He had two days left to decide.

But Franklin was too busy to think about the toy drive.

He played the recorder in the school concert, made a card for Mr. Owl and wrote a holiday story.

"I'll pick a toy after school," he promised himself.

When Franklin got home, there was a gift for him under the tree. It was from Great Aunt Harriet.

Franklin was so excited that he forgot all about choosing a gift for the toy drive.

Franklin squeezed the present and shook it.

"No peeking," laughed his mother.

"Do you know what it is?" asked Franklin eagerly.

"It must be something special." His mother smiled. "Great Aunt Harriet always gives presents that mean something to you and to her."

"Like last year," said Franklin.

Great Aunt Harriet knew that he loved to put on plays. And she gave him two puppets that had been hers when she was little. It was one of Franklin's best presents ever.

The next day at school, the collection box
was brimming.

"You've all been very generous," said Mr. Owl.
"Do you know that your gift might be the only
one somebody receives this holiday?"

Franklin gulped. He'd never thought of that.
He had to bring a present tomorrow!

Franklin raced home after school and looked through his toys again.

Somebody else might love Elephant, but she was worn from so much hugging.

And Franklin wasn't sure that the red car went fast enough.

Franklin was upset. At first, all of his toys had seemed too special to give away. Now, nothing seemed special enough.

Franklin played with his puppets and thought about how Great Aunt Harriet chose her gifts.

"The best presents are special to give and to receive," he whispered.

Then Franklin saw his marble collection and he knew that the marbles were special enough for the toy drive.

Franklin polished them and put them into a soft purple bag.

He wrapped the present and made a gift tag that read:

These are lucky marbles.
Merry Christmas.

The next morning, Franklin put his present
on top of the collection box.

Then Franklin and his friends hauled the
box to the big tree at the Town Hall.

They placed each present under the tree.

Franklin knew he would miss his marble
collection. Still, he didn't feel at all sad. Instead,
he felt good all over.

On Christmas Eve, Great Aunt Harriet came to visit and Franklin was allowed to open her present.

He ripped off the paper.

"It's perfect!" said Franklin. "Thank you."

Great Aunt Harriet beamed. She had made a stage for Franklin's puppet shows.

"Now open yours," Franklin insisted.

Great Aunt Harriet unwrapped her gift slowly and carefully.

Inside was a play, written by Franklin and dedicated to her.

"This is my best Christmas present ever," said Great Aunt Harriet.

Franklin got that good-all-over feeling one more time.

Franklin's Thanksgiving

FRANKLIN liked everything about Thanksgiving.
He liked eating pumpkin-fly pie and cranberry jelly.
He liked making cornucopias and cornhusk dolls.
But most of all, he liked having his Grandma and
Grandpa come for dinner. It was the family tradition,
and Franklin could hardly wait.

A week before Thanksgiving, a postcard arrived from Franklin's grandparents.

"Oh dear," sighed Franklin's mother. "Grandma and Grandpa can't make it back for the holiday."

"But they have to!" cried Franklin. "They're always here for Thanksgiving."

Franklin's mother gave him a hug. "There will still be the four of us," she said.

"It won't be the same," Franklin grumbled.

Over the next few days, Franklin was so busy that he didn't have much time to think about Grandma and Grandpa. He helped his mother pick apples and make applesauce. He helped his father dig up vegetables and store them in the cellar. Franklin and Bear helped Harriet and Beatrice pick berries and gather nuts.

In the gardens and orchards, forests and fields, everyone was bringing in the harvest.

105

Franklin counted all the jars of jams and preserves.

"I think this year was the most bountiful ever," announced his father. "We could feed the whole town!"

"I just wish we could feed Grandma and Grandpa," sighed Franklin.

His mother agreed. "We'll miss having company," she said.

At school, Franklin's class made a harvest quilt and learned how the early settlers celebrated Thanksgiving.

"What are you doing for Thanksgiving, Mr. Owl?" asked Franklin.

"I'll have dinner with my mother," he replied. "Our relatives can't visit this year."

"Ours neither," said Franklin.

Then he had an idea. He invited Mr. Owl and his mother for dinner.

"It's all right with my parents," Franklin explained. "They want company."

"Well, thank you, Franklin," said Mr. Owl. "We'd be delighted to come."

Franklin smiled. This would be a wonderful surprise for his parents.

At home, Franklin's mother looked at the berry pies cooling on the windowsill.

She had an idea.

She walked over to Bear's house and invited the whole family for Thanksgiving.

"It will be a wonderful surprise for everyone," she explained.

In the garden, Franklin's father waved to Mr. Mole.

"Are you going to your sister's for Thanksgiving?" he asked.

"Not this year," replied Mr. Mole. "With my broken ankle, I can't go far."

Franklin's father had an idea. He invited Mr. Mole for dinner.

"It will be a wonderful surprise for everyone," he explained.

After school, Franklin went home with Moose.
That's when he had another idea.

It was the Moose family's first Thanksgiving in
Woodland. Franklin invited them for dinner.

"It's all right with my parents," he explained.
"They want company."

"We'd be delighted," replied Mrs. Moose.

Franklin smiled. His surprise was getting bigger
and bigger.

On Thanksgiving morning, Franklin got up early
to help with dinner. He stirred soup and shucked corn.
Then he set the table for nine.

Franklin's father counted the place settings. He
shook his head and reset the table for five.

Franklin's mother looked at the table. She was
puzzled, but she added three more place settings.

And everyone took turns peeking out the window,
watching for the surprise guests.

Mr. Owl and his mother were the first to arrive.

"Surprise!" Franklin shouted to his parents.

"This *is* a surprise!" they exclaimed.

Then Franklin saw the Bear family and Mr. Mole.

Now everyone was surprised.

All the guests crowded inside, holding platters and bowls heaped high with food.

Franklin and his parents laughed and tried to explain what had happened.

"Well, we sure have plenty to eat," declared Franklin's mother. "We just don't have plenty of room."

Franklin knew they had a big problem.

The Moose family hadn't arrived yet.

Franklin looked around. There wasn't one bit of room inside. But outside ...

Suddenly, Franklin knew what to do.

Moose and his family arrived as all the others came out the door. Everyone carried food and dishes, tables and chairs.

"What's going on?" asked Moose.

"We're eating our Thanksgiving dinner in the field," answered Bear.

"Just like the early settlers," said Franklin.

It was a wonderful afternoon. Everyone ate lots of good food, and everyone said how thankful they were for good friends and family.

Franklin was thankful for three helpings of pumpkin-fly pie.

"I'm eating Grandma and Grandpa's share," he explained.

Soon the sun was setting and it was time to go home. "This was a wonderful day," said Franklin's mother. Franklin agreed. "Let's do it again next year!" he said. Everyone laughed and cheered.

Grandma and Grandpa phoned later that night, and Franklin told them all about the new Thanksgiving tradition. They promised that next year they wouldn't miss it for anything.

Franklin smiled. He might not get three helpings of pumpkin-fly pie next year, but he knew he'd still be thankful.